Published by Hachette Partworks Ltd.
ISBN: 978-1-910360-43-9
Date of Printing: March 2016
Printed in Romania by Canale

DISNEY · PIXAR
THE GOOD DINOSAUR

DISNEY · PIXAR

H hachette

What if, sixty-five million years ago, the giant asteroid that was heading for Earth suddenly changed course and missed our planet? This is the story of what might have happened...

Millions of years after that asteroid hurtled through space, dinosaurs were still on Earth, many of them working on the land.

Henry, an apatosaurus, lived at the foot of Clawtooth Mountain with his wife, Ida. They had three children; Libby, Buck and Arlo, the littlest.

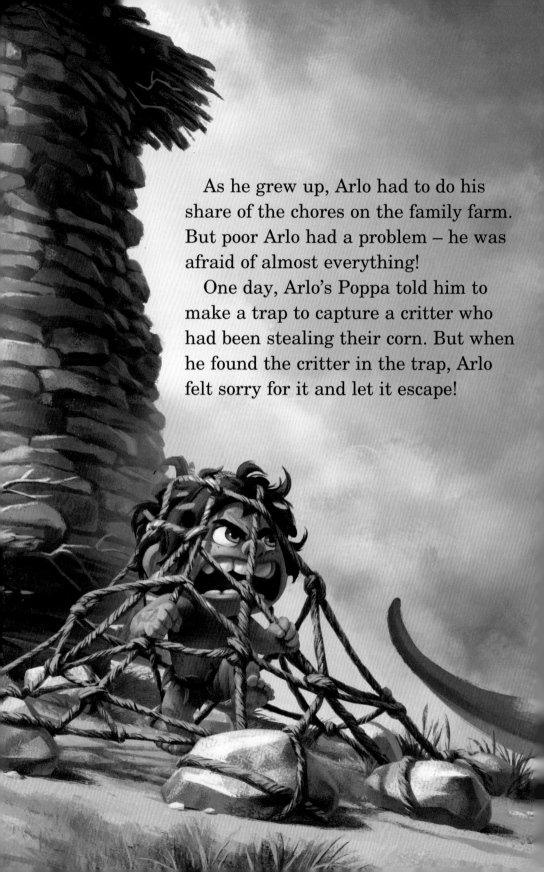

As he grew up, Arlo had to do his share of the chores on the family farm. But poor Arlo had a problem – he was afraid of almost everything!

One day, Arlo's Poppa told him to make a trap to capture a critter who had been stealing their corn. But when he found the critter in the trap, Arlo felt sorry for it and let it escape!

Poppa was angry that the critter had escaped. He chased after it, just as a terrible storm broke. As the river rose, Poppa managed to push Arlo onto a safe ledge. But he slipped into the raging river and was swept away.

"Poppa!" cried Arlo, terrified.

Without Poppa, life on the farm was hard for the family. One day, when Arlo was at the corn silo, he came face to face with a critter – it was the same one that Poppa and Arlo had trapped!

"It's all your fault!" yelled Arlo. "My poppa would still be alive if it weren't for you!"

Arlo grabbed the critter, but as they struggled, they both fell into the river.

"Help! Momma!" cried Arlo as the fast-flowing water swept him away, far from the shore.

Finally, Arlo
washed up on
a rocky shore.
Where was he? How
would he get home?
He climbed up a steep
cliff and when he got to the
top, he saw the critter.

"Go away!" he shouted angrily.
The critter ran off.

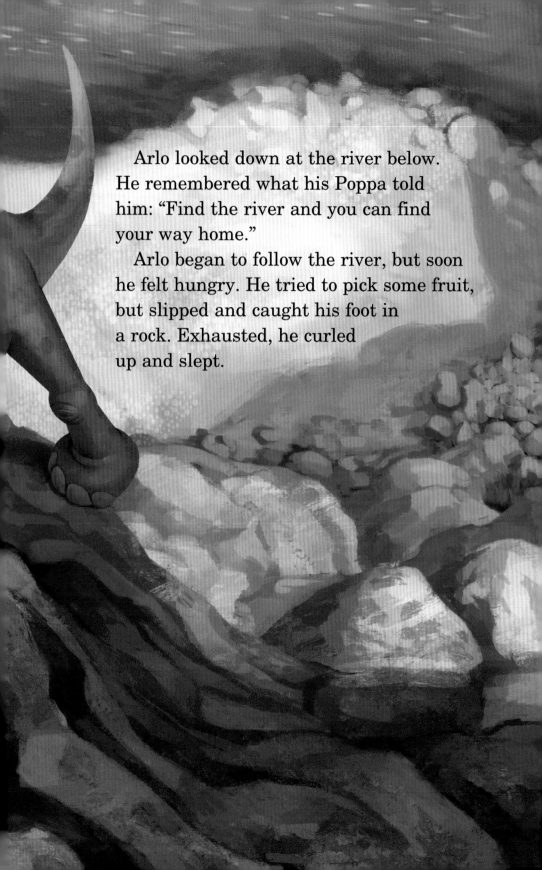

Arlo looked down at the river below. He remembered what his Poppa told him: "Find the river and you can find your way home."

Arlo began to follow the river, but soon he felt hungry. He tried to pick some fruit, but slipped and caught his foot in a rock. Exhausted, he curled up and slept.

Later, Arlo awoke to find that his foot was no longer trapped. And the critter had brought him delicious berries to eat! Arlo still didn't trust the critter, but when it scared away a fierce snake, he had to admit it was a brave little thing.

He decided to call the critter Spot.

That night, Arlo and Spot found a cave by the river to sleep in.

"I miss my family," said Arlo sadly.

Spot hugged Arlo's leg to comfort him. Then he lifted his head and began to howl sorrowfully. He was missing his family, too. Arlo joined in and, in the moonlight, the two new friends howled for their lost loved ones.

A few days later, Arlo and Spot met a
T. rex called Butch and his two sons, Nash
and Ramsey. They were ranchers, searching
for their lost herd of longhorns.

Suddenly, they were attacked by a pack
of raptors. Arlo pushed aside his fears and
joined the T. rexes to drive the attackers off.

That night, everyone sat round the camp fire as the T. rexes told tales of their daring adventures.

"You guys would've liked my Poppa," said Arlo. "He wasn't scared of anything."

Arlo sighed. "I'm done with being scared."

"You can't get rid of fear, kid," said Butch to Arlo. "But you can get through it. You can find out what you're made of."

The next day, Arlo and Spot left their new friends and headed for home.

But there was more danger in store!
As a storm brewed, a gang of fearsome
pterodactyls swooped out of the sky. They
caught hold of Spot and tried to carry him
off, but Arlo raced to the rescue. With a
terrifying roar, he charged at the raiders,
scaring them off.

On the last day of Arlo and Spot's journey, they met a group of humans.

Arlo knew what he had to do. He didn't want to lose Spot, but the boy needed a family. The friends said a sad goodbye.

At first, Momma didn't recognise the tall,
confident stranger who looked just like Poppa.
And then she realised – it was her lost son!
At last, Arlo had found his way home.